For Mason and Sophie,
may your deepest wishes come true —A.J.I.

For Emily —K.A.

THIS IS A BORZOI BOOK PUBLISHED BY ALFRED A. KNOPF

Text copyright © 2023 by A. J. Irving

Jacket art and interior illustrations copyright © 2023 by Kip Alizadeh

All rights reserved. Published in the United States by Alfred A. Knopf,

an imprint of Random House Children's Books, a division of Penguin Random House LLC, New York.

Knopf, Borzoi Books, and the colophon are registered trademarks of Penguin Random House LLC.

Visit us on the Web! rhcbooks.com

Educators and librarians, for a variety of teaching tools, visit us at RHTeachersLibrarians.com

Library of Congress Cataloging-in-Publication Data is available upon request.

ISBN 978-0-593-43044-6 (trade) — ISBN 978-0-593-43045-3 (lib. bdg.) — ISBN 978-0-593-43046-0 (ebook)

The text of this book is set in 15-point Meta Pro Medium.

The illustrations were created using scanned-in pencil lines, scanned-in textures, and Photoshop colors.

Book design by Sarah Hokanson

MANUFACTURED IN CHINA 10 9 8 7 6 5 4 3 2 1 First Edition

THE WISHING FLOWER

WRITTEN BY A. J. Irving

ILLUSTRATED BY Kip Alizadeh

Alfred A. Knopf New York

Birdie loved books and bugs and birds and stars,
but most of all, she loved to watch her wishes soar.

Every time Birdie found a wishing flower, she closed her eyes and blew.

But Birdie worried her wish would never come true.

Birdie felt inside out at home and at school.
Quiet as starlight and shy like a pill bug,
Birdie curled up in the pages of her books.

She never asked the other kids to jump rope or swing, but everything changed the day . . .

. . . the new
girl came.

Sunny had freckles
like constellations and
a nature name.

She was a reader and a rescuer.

She even drew a bluebird
during art.
Birdie drew a sun.

When Sunny smiled, two dragonflies played tag in Birdie's tummy.
When Sunny waved, Birdie's heart fluttered as fast as a hummingbird's wings.
When Sunny said hello, Birdie wanted to sing hello right back.

But instead, Birdie blushed when Sunny sat next to her at lunch.

At recess, Birdie searched for the biggest wishing flower.
Now, she longed to be brave.

But just before she made her wish, the bell rang.

The rest of the day was filled with surprises.

"Red Rover, Red Rover, send Birdie on over!" Sunny called.

Birdie grinned, spread her wings, and flew.
Her heart ballooned like a parachute.

And her bravery grew.

Sunny smiled and Birdie waved. "Sunny!" Birdie sang. "Want to play?"

After school, they skipped to the playground hand in hand.

Birdie and Sunny jumped in sync.

They braided each other's hair.

Birdie and Sunny cartwheeled, crashed, and laughed.
They watched the geese disappear.

Together, they soared so high their toes kissed the clouds.

"It's a little squished," Birdie said.
"Let's make a wish," Sunny said.

Birdie and Sunny closed their eyes and blew.
"Mine already came true."
"Mine, too."